The Urbana Free Library

To renew: call **217-367-4057**
or go to **urbanafreelibrary.org**
and select **My Account**

Dear Parents, Educators, and Guardians,

Thank you for helping your child dive into this book with us. We believe in the power of books to transport readers to other worlds, expand their horizons, and help them discover cultures and experiences that may differ from their own.

We also believe that books should inspire young readers to imagine a diverse world that includes them, a world in which they can see themselves as the heroes of their own stories.

These are our hopes for all our readers. So come on. Dive into reading and explore the world with us!

From,
Your friends at Lee & Low

Music Time

Henry   Lily   Mei   Pablo   Padma

by **Gwendolyn Hooks**

illustrated by **Shirley Ng-Benitez**

Lee & Low Books Inc. New York

To Leslie, Eddy, and Alison—for bringing music into our home—G.H.

To Mrs. Franke, Mrs. Sodergren, and all the music teachers—
thank you for spreading peace through music!—S.N-B.

LEE & LOW BOOKS Inc., 95 Madison Avenue, New York, NY 10016
leeandlow.com
Book design by Kimi Weart
Book production by The Kids at Our House
The illustrations are rendered in watercolor and enhanced digitally
Manufactured in China by Imago, February 2017
Printed on paper from responsible sources
(hc) 10 9 8 7 6 5 4 3 2 1
(pb) 10 9 8 7 6 5 4 3 2 1
First Edition

Library of Congress Cataloging-in-Publication Data
Names: Hooks, Gwendolyn, author. | Ng-Benitez, Shirley, illustrator.
Title: Music time / by Gwendolyn Hooks ; illustrated by Shirley Ng-Benitez.
Description: First edition. | New York: Lee & Low Books, [2017]
Series: Dive into reading; 4 | Summary: "Henry's drum practice at home
is too loud so he goes outside and when he sees his friends playing jump
rope he figures out a way to play drums and play with his friends."
Identifiers: LCCN 2016028089 | ISBN 9781620143438 (hardcover: alk. paper)
ISBN 9781620143445 (pbk.: alk. paper)
Subjects: | CYAC: Drum—Fiction. | Play—Fiction. | Friendship—Fiction.
Classification: LCC PZ7.H76635 Mu 2017 | DDC [E]—dc23
LC record available at https://lccn.loc.gov/2016028089

Contents

Rock Star

Henry played his drums.
Henry played his drums loudly.

BOOM, BOOM, BAM!

"HENRY!" said his mom.
"You're playing too loudly."

"Rock stars play loudly,"
said Henry.
"I have work," said Henry's mom.
"Please don't play loudly."

Henry played his drums quietly.
Then he pretended to play
for a big show.

Henry played his drums louder.
People clapped.
Henry played louder and louder.

"HENRY!" called his mom.
"You're playing too loudly."
Henry wanted to be quiet
for his mom.
But he wanted to play
his drums too.

"I'll go outside and play
my old drum," said Henry.
"Great idea," said his mom.

Freeze Dance

Henry sat on the steps
with his old drum.

His friends Pablo, Mei, Lily, and
Padma were playing jump rope.

"Hi, Henry," said Mei.
"Do you want to play?"

Henry wanted to play
with his friends.
But he wanted to play
his drum too.

"I have an idea," said Henry.
"Let's play freeze dance."

"What's freeze dance?" asked Lily.
"I play the drum and you dance,"
said Henry.
"When I stop playing,
you stop dancing."

Henry played his drum.
His friends did silly dances.
Then Henry stopped playing.

Lily, Pablo, and Mei stopped.
But Padma didn't stop.
"Padma, you're out!" said Henry.
"Okay," said Padma.

Henry played his drum again.
BOOM, BOOM, BAM!

This time Pablo was out.

Henry played his drum
again and again.
His friends did silly dances
again and again.

Then it was time for dinner.
Everyone went home.

Dance Party

After dinner Henry's mom
still had to work.

Henry looked for something
quiet to do.

"Henry, you're so quiet,"
said his mom.
"Are you okay?"

"Yes," said Henry.
"I'm drawing a picture."

"I'm done with work,"
said Henry's mom.
"Want to play?"

"Yes," said Henry.
"Want to dance with me?"
"Yes!" said his mom.

Henry's mom turned on some music.
Henry and his mom danced.

They did silly dances.
They danced until it was time
for Henry to go to bed.

☆ **Activity** ☆

Do you want to play some music?
Here is how to make your own drum.

You will need:

- A round can with a lid, such as an oatmeal box or a coffee container
- Construction paper or wrapping paper
- Scissors
- Glue
- Chopsticks or short, strong twigs

1. Decorate the can with construction paper or wrapping paper.

2. Cut out paper shapes and glue them onto the can.

3. Use the chopsticks or twigs as drumsticks to play a beat on the lid of the can.

4. You can also beat the lid with your hands.

Gwendolyn Hooks has written several children's books, including Bebop Books' *Can I Have a Pet?* and Lee & Low's *Tiny Stitches*. When she was a child, her family moved often, and her first stop in every new city was the library. Hooks lives in Oklahoma City, Oklahoma, with her family.

Shirley Ng-Benitez creates illustrations with watercolor, gouache, pencil, and digital techniques. She also loves to create 3-D creatures from clay and fabric. She lives in the Bay Area of California with her husband, their two daughters, and their pup.

Read More About Henry and His Friends!